THE BROWNIE OF THE
BLACK HAGGS

BY

JAMES HOGG

British Library Cataloguing-in-Publication Data
A catalogue record for this book is available from the
British Library

CONTENTS

JAMES HOGG

James Hogg was born near Ettrick, Scotland in 1770. James had almost no formal education, and lived in grinding poverty as a shepherd. His employer, seeing how hard he was working to improve himself, offered to help by lending him books. Using these, Hogg taught himself to read and write, and was fully literate by the age of 14. In 1801, aged 31, Hogg visited Edinburgh for the first time. His first collection of poetry, *The Mountain Bard*, was published in 1807, but made little impact. However, his epic prose-poem, *The Queen's Wake* (1813), was a great success, transforming him quickly into a well-known literary figure. Despite being mocked somewhat for his rustic accent and appearance, Hogg was recruited by William Blackwood to the staff of his *Blackwood's Magazine*.

Blackwood's – partly through its reputation for ruffling public feathers – became one of the most well-known magazines of its day. Indeed, it was Hogg's association with *Blackwood's* 'Noctes Ambrosianae' series of satirical sketches (in which 'Ettrick Shepherd' starred as a thinly veiled version of Hogg himself), perhaps more than his own work, which secured his contemporary fame. However, it wasn't exactly the type of fame Hogg had been after. 'Ettrick Shepherd' was a rural simpleton who in fact probably intensified Hogg's exclusion from Edinburgh's high society, and a combination of his own dissatisfaction and the magazine staff's cliquishness saw him increasingly left out of *Blackwood's* inner circle.

By 1824, Hogg found himself out of favour in Edinburgh, in his fifties but with a young family, and desperate for money to save his failing farm. In this year, he produced what is now seen as his masterpiece: *The Private Memoirs and Confessions of a Justified Sinner*. The novel was virtually ignored by reviewers of the day, and underwent a century or so of critical neglect, but is now regarded by many as something of a forgotten classic. In 1924, in what might be regarded as sparking *Justified Sinners* critical revival, Nobel Prize-winning French author André Gidesaid of the novel that "It is long since I can remember being so taken hold of, so voluptuously tormented by any book."

Hogg died at his home in 1835, aged 64. William Wordsworth, who composed his eulogy, dubbed Hogg "undoubtedly a man of original genius, but of coarse manners and low and offensive opinions." Today, Hogg's revival continues; his story 'The Brownie Of The Black Haggs' was dramatised for BBC Radio 4 in 2003, and more recently the villain of that story, Merodach, appeared as the villain in a 2010 Doctor Who audiobook, *Night's Black Agents*.

THE BROWNIE OF THE BLACK HAGGS

SIR ARTHUR CONAN DOYLE

When the Sprots were Lairds of Wheelhope, which is now a long time ago, there was one of the ladies who was very badly spoken of in the country. People did not just openly assert that Lady Wheelhope (for every landward laird's wife was then styled Lady) was a witch, but every one had an aversion even at hearing her named; and when by chance she happened to be mentioned, old men would shake their heads and say, 'Ah! let us alane o' her! The less ye meddle wi' her the better.' Old wives would give over spinning, and, as a pretence for hearing what might be said about her, poke in the fire with the tongs, cocking up their ears all the while; and then, after some meaning coughs, hcms, and haws, would haply say, 'Hech-wow, sirs! An a' be true that's said!' or something equally wise and decisive.

In short, Lady Wheelhope was accounted a very bad woman. She was an inexorable tyrant in her family, quarrelled with her servants, often cursing them, striking them, and turning them away; especially if they were religious, for she could not endure people of that character, but charged them with every thing bad. Whenever she found out that any of the servant men of the Laird's establishment were religious, she gave them up to the military, and got them shot; and several girls that were regular in their devotions, she was supposed to have got rid of by poison. She was certainly a wicked woman, else many good people were mistaken in her character; and the poor persecuted Covenanters were obliged to unite in their prayers against her.

As for the Laird, he was a big, dun-faced, pluffy body, that cared neither for good nor evil, and did not well know the one from the other. He laughed at his lady's tantrums and barley-hoods; and the greater the rage that she got into, the Laird thought it the better sport. One day, when two maid-servants came running to him, in great agitation, and told him that his lady had felled one of their companions, the Laird laughed heartily, and said he did not doubt it.

'Why, sir, how can you laugh?' said they. 'The poor girl is killed.'

'Very likely, very likely,' said the Laird. 'Well, it will teach her to take care who she angers again.'

'And, sir, your lady will be hanged.'

'Very likely; well, it will teach her not to strike so rashly again – Ha, ha, ha! Will it not, Jessy?'

But when this same Jessy died suddenly one morning,

the Laird was greatly confounded, and seemed dimly to comprehend that there had been unfair play going. There was little doubt that she was taken off by poison; but whether the Lady did it through jealously or not, was never divulged; but it greatly bamboozled and astonished the poor Laird, for his nerves failed him, and his whole frame became paralytic. He seems to have been exactly in the same state of mind with a colley that I once had. He was extremely fond of the gun as long as I did not kill anything with it (there being no game laws in Ettrick Forrest in those days), he got a grand chase after the hares when I missed them. But there was one day that I chanced for a marvel to shoot one dead, a few paces before his nose. I'll never forget the astonishment that the poor beast manifested. He stared one while at the gun, and another while at the dead hare, and seemed to be drawing the conclusion, that if the case stood thus, there was no creature sure of its life. Finally, he took his tail between his legs and ran away home, and never would face a gun all his life again.

So was it precisely with Laird Sprot of Wheelhope. As long as his lady's wrath produced only noise and uproar among the servants, he thought it fine sport; but when he saw what he believed the dreadful effects of it, he became like a barrel organ out of tune, and could only discourse one note, which he did to every one he met. 'I wish she mayna hae gotten something she had been the waur of.' This note he repeated early and late, night and day, sleeping and waking, alone and in company, from the moment that Jessy died till she was buried; and on going to the churchyard as chief mourner, he whispered it to her relatives by the way. When they came to the grave, he took his stand at the head, nor would he give place to the girl's father; but there he stood, like a huge post, as though he neither saw nor heard; and when he had lowered her head into the grave and dropped the cord, he slowly lifted his hat with one hand, wiped his dim eyes with the back of the other, and said, in a deep tremulous tone, 'Poor lassie! I wish she didna get something she had been the waur of.'

This death made a great noise among the common people; but there was little protection for the life of the subject in those days; and provided a man or woman was a real Anti-Covenanter, they might kill a good many without being quarrelled for it. So there was no one to take cognizance of the circumstances relating to the death of poor Jessy.

After this the Lady walked softly for the space of two or three years. She saw that she had rendered herself odious, and had entirely lost her husband's countenance, which she liked worst of all. But the evil propensity could not be overcome; and a poor boy, whom the Laird out of sheer compassion had taken into his service, being found dead one morning, the country people could no longer be restrained; so they went in a body to the Sheriff, and insisted on an investigation. It was proved that she detested the boy, had often threatened him, and had given him brose and butter the afternoon before he died; but notwithstanding of all this, the cause was ultimately dismissed, and the pursuers fined.

No one can tell to what height of wickedness she might now have proceeded, had not a check of a very singular kind been laid upon her. Among the servants that came home at the next term, was one who called himself Merodach; and a strange person he was. He had the form of a boy, but the features of one a hundred years old, save that his eyes had a brilliancy and restlessness, which were very extraordinary, bearing a strong resemblance to the eyes of a well-known species of monkey. He was forward and perverse, and disregarded the pleasure or displeasure of any person; but he performed his work well and with apparent ease. From the moment he entered the house, the Lady conceived a mortal antipathy against him, and besought the Laird to turn him away. But the Laird would not consent; he never turned away any servant, and moreover he had hired this fellow for a trivial wage, and he neither wanted activity nor perseverance. The natural consequence of this refusal was, that the Lady instantly set herself to embitter Merodach's life as much as possible, in order to get early quit of a domestic every way so disagreeable. Her hatred of him was not like a common antipathy entertained by one human being against another – she hated him as one might hate a toad or an adder; and his occupation of jotteryman (as the Laird termed his servant of all work) keeping him always about her hand, it must have proved highly annoying.

She scolded him, she raged at him; but he only mocked her wrath, and giggled and laughed at her, with the most provoking derision. She tried to fell him again and again, but never, with all her address, could she hit him; and never did she make a blow at him, that she did not repent it. She was heavy and unwieldy, and he as quick in his motions as a monkey; besides, he generally contrived that she should be in such an ungovernable rage, that when she flew at him, she hardly knew what she was doing. At one time she guided her blow towards him, and he at the same instant avoided it with such dexterity that she knocked down the chief hind, or foresman; and then Merodach giggled so heartily, that, lifting the kitchen poker, she threw it at him with a full design of knocking out his brains; but the missile only broke every article of crockery on the kitchen dresser.

She then hasted to the Laird, crying bitterly, and telling him she would not suffer that wretch Merodach, as she called him, to stay another night in the family.

'Why, then, put him away, and trouble me no more about

him,' said the Laird.

'Put him away!' exclaimed she, 'I have already ordered him away a hundred times, and charged him never to let me see his horrible face again; but he only grins, and answers with some intolerable piece of impertinence.'

The pertinacity of the fellow amused the Laird; his dim eyes turned upwards into his head with delight; he then looked two ways at once, turned round his back, and laughed till the tears ran down his dun cheeks; but he could only articulate, 'You're fitted now.'

The Lady's agony of rage still increasing from his derision, she upbraided the Laird bitterly, and said he was not worthy the name of man, if he did not turn away that pestilence, after the way he had abused her.

'Why, Shusy, my dear, what has he done to you?'

'What done to me! has he not caused me to knock down John Thomson? and I do not know if ever he will come to life again!'

'Have you felled your favourite John Thomson?' said the Laird, laughing more heartily than before; 'you might have done a worse deed than that.'

'And has he not broke every plate and dish on the whole dresser?' continued the Lady; 'and for all this devastation, he only mocks at my displeasure – absolutely mocks me – and if you do not have him turned away, and hanged or shot for his deeds, you are not worthy the name of man.'

'O alack! What a devastation among the cheena metal!' said the Laird; and calling on Merodach, he said, 'Tell me, thou evil Merodach of Babylon, how thou daredst knock down thy Lady's favourite servant, John Thomson?'

'Not I, your honour. It was my Lady herself, who got into such a furious rage at me, that she mistook her man, and felled Mr Thomson; and the good man's skull is fractured.'

'That was very odd,' said the Laird, chuckling; 'I do not comprehend it. But then, what set you on smashing all my Lady's delft and cheena ware? – That was a most infamous and provoking action.'

'It was she herself, your honour. Sorry would I be to break one dish belonging to the house. I take all the house servants to witness, that my Lady smashed all the dishes with a poker; and now lays the blame on me!'

The Laird turned his dim eyes on his Lady, who was crying with vexation and rage, and seemed meditating another personal attack on the culprit, which he did not at all appear to shun, but rather to court. She, however, vented her wrath in threatenings of the most deep and desperate revenge, the creature all the while assuring her that she would be foiled, and that in all her encounters and contest with him, she would uniformly come to the worst; he was resolved to do his duty, and there before his master he defied her.

The Laird thought more than he considered it prudent to reveal; he had little doubt that his wife would find some means of wreaking her vengeance on the object of her displeasure; and he shuddered when he recollected on who had taken 'something that she had been the waur of.'

In a word, the Lady of Wheelhope's inveterate malignity against this one object, was like the rod of Moses, that swallowed up the rest of the serpents. All her wicked and evil propensities seemed to be superseded if not utterly absorbed by it. The rest of the family now lived in comparative peace and quietness; for early and late her malevolence was venting itself against the jotteryman, and against him alone. It was a delirium of hatred and vengeance, on which the whole bent and bias of her inclination was set. She could not stay from the creature's presence, or, in the intervals when absent from him, she spent her breath in curses and execrations; and then, not able to rest, she ran again to seek him, her eyes gleaming with the anticipated delights of vengeance, while, ever and anon, all the ridicule and the harm rebounded on herself.

Was it not strange that she could not get quit of this sole annoyance of her life? One would have thought she easily might. But by this time there was nothing farther from her wishes; she wanted vengeance, full, adequate, and delicious vengeance, on her audacious opponent. But he was a strange and terrible creature, and the means of retaliation constantly came, as it were, to his hand.

Bread and sweet milk was the only fare that Merodach cared for, and having bargained for that, he would not want it, though he often got it with a curse and with ill will. The Lady having, upon one occasion, intentionally kept back his wonted allowance for some days, on the Sabbath morning following, she set him down a bowl of rich sweet milk, well drugged with a deadly poison; and then she lingered in a little ante-room to watch the success of her grand plot, and prevent any other creature from tasting of the potion. Merodach came in, and the housemaid said to him, 'There is your breakfast, creature.'

'Oho! my Lady has been liberal this morning,' said he; 'but I am beforehand with her. Here, little Missie, you seem very hungry today – take you my breakfast.' And with that he set the beverage down to the Lady's little favourite spaniel. It so happened that the Lady's only son came at that instant into the ante-room seeking her, and teasing his mamma about something, which withdrew her attention from the hall-table for a space. When she looked again, and saw Missie lapping up the sweet milk, she burst from her hiding-place like a fury, screaming as if her head had been on fire, kicked the remainder of its contents against the wall, and lifting Missie in her bosom, retreated hastily, crying all the way.

'Ha, ha, ha – I have you now!' cried Merodach, as she vanished from the hall.

Poor Missie died immediately, and very privately; indeed, she would have died and been buried, and never one have seen her, save her mistress, had not Merodach, by a luck that never failed him, looked over the wall of the flower garden, just as his lady was laying her favourite in a grave of her own digging. She, not perceiving her tormentor, plied on at her task, apostrophising the insensate little carcass – 'Ah! poor dear little creature, thou hast had a hard fortune, and has drank of the bitter potion that was not intended for thee; but he shall drink it three times double for thy sake!'

'Is that little Missie?' said the eldritch voice of the jotteryman, close at the lady's ear. She uttered a loud scream, and sank down on the bank. 'Alack for poor Missie!' continued the creature in a tone of mockery, 'my heart is sorry for Missie. What has befallen her – whose breakfast cup did she drink?'

'Hence with thee, fiend!' cried the Lady; 'what right hast thou to intrude on thy mistress's privacy? Thy turn is coming yet; or may the nature of woman change within me!'

'It is changed already,' said the creature, grinning with delight; 'I have thee now, I have thee now! And were it no to show my superiority over thee, which I do every hour, I should soon see thee strapped like a mad cat, or a worrying bratch. What wilt thou try next?'

'I will cut thy throat, and if I die for it, will rejoice in the deed; a deed of charity to all that dwell on the face of the earth.'

'I have warned thee before, dame, and I now warn thee again, that all thy mischief meditated against me will fall double on thine own head.'

'I want none of your warning, fiendish cur. Hence with your elvish face, and take care of yourself.'

It would be too disgusting and horrible to relate or read all the incidents that fell out between this unaccountable couple. Their enmity against each other had no end, and no mitigation; and scarcely a single day passed over on which the Lady's acts of malevolent ingenuity did not terminate fatally for some favourite thing of her own. Scarcely was there a thing, animate or inanimate, on which she set a value, left to her, that was not destroyed; and yet scarcely one hour or minute could she remain absent from her tormentor, and all the while, it seems, solely for the purpose of tormenting him. While all the rest of the establishment enjoyed peace and quietness from the fury of their termagant dame, matters still grew worse and worse between the fascinated pair. The Lady haunted the menial, in the same manner as the raven haunts the eagle, for a perpetual quarrel, though the former knows that in every encounter she is to come off the loser. Noises were heard on the stairs by night, and it was whispered among the servants, that the lady had been seeking Merodach's chamber, on some horrible intent. Several of them would have sworn that they had seen her passing and repassing on the stair after midnight, when all was quiet; but then it was likewise well known that Merodach slept with well-fastened doors, and a companion in another bed in the same room, whose bed, too, was nearest the door. Nobody cared much what became of the jotteryman, for he was an unsocial and disagreeable person; but someone told him what they had seen, and hinted a suspicion of the Lady's intent. But the creature only bit his upper lip, winked with his eyes, and said, 'She had better let that alone; she will be the first to rue that.'

Not long after this, to the horror of the family and the whole countryside, the Laird's only son was found murdered in his bed one morning, under circumstances that manifested the most fiendish cruelty and inveteracy on the part of his destroyer. As soon as the atrocious act was divulged the Lady fell into convulsions, and lost her reason; and happy had it been for her had she never recovered the use of it, for there was blood upon her hand, which she took no care to conceal, and there was little doubt that it was the blood of her own innocent and beloved boy, the sole heir and hope of the family.

This blow deprived the Laird of all power of action; but the lady had a brother, a man of the law, who came and instantly proceeded to an investigation of this unaccountable murder. Before the Sheriff arrived, the housekeeper took the Lady's brother aside, and told him he had better not go on with the scrutiny, for she was sure the crime would be brought home to her unfortunate mistress; and after examining into several corroborative circumstances, and viewing the state of the raving maniac, with the blood on her hand and arm, he made the investigation a very short one, declaring the domestics all exculpated.

The Laird attended his boy's funeral, and laid his head in the grave, but appeared exactly like a man walking in a trance, an automaton, without feelings or sensations, oftentimes gazing at the funeral procession, as on something he could not comprehend. And when the death-bell of the parish church fell a-tolling, as the corpse approached the kirk-stile, he cast a dim eye up towards the belfry, and said hastily, 'What, what's that? Och ay, we're just in time, just in time.' And often was he hammering over the name of 'Evil Merodach, King of Babylon', to himself. He seemed to have some farfetched conception that his unaccountable jotteryman was in some way connected with the death of his only son, and other lesser calamities, although the evidence in favour of Merodach's innocence was as usual quite decisive.

This grievous mistake of Lady Wheelhope can only be accounted for, by supposing her in a state of derangement, or rather under some evil influence, over which she had no control; and to a person in such a state, the mistake was not so very unnatural. The mansion-house of Wheelhope was old and irregular. The stair had four acute turns, and four landing-places, all the same. In the uppermost chamber slept the two domestics – Merodach in the bed farthest in, and in the chamber immediately below that, which was exactly similar, slept the young Laird and his tutor, the former in the bed farthest in; and thus, in the turmoil of her wild and raging passions, her own hand made herself childless.

Merodach was expelled by the family forthwith, but refused to accept of his wages which the man of law pressed upon him, for fear of further mischief; but he went away in apparent sullenness and discontent, no one knowing whither.

When his dismissal was announced to the Lady, who was watched day and night in her chamber, the news had such an effect on her, that her whole frame seemed electrified: the horrors of remorse vanished, and another passion, which I neither can comprehend nor define, took the sole possession of her distempered spirit. 'He *must* not go! – He *shall* not go!' she exclaimed. 'No, no, no – he shall not – he shall not – he shall not!' and then she instantly set herself about making ready to follow him, uttering all the while the most diabolical expressions, indicative of anticipated vengeance. 'Oh, could I but snap his nerves one by one, and birl among his vitals! Could I but slice his heart off piecemeal in small messes, and see his blood lopper, and bubble, and spin away in purple slays: and then to see him grin, and grin, and grin, and grin! Oh – oh – oh – How beautiful and grand a sight it would be to see him grin, and grin, and grin!' And in such a style would she run on for hours together.

She thought of nothing, she spake of nothing, but the discarded jotteryman, whom most people now began to regard as a creature that was 'not canny'. They had seen him eat and drink, and work, like other people; still he had that about him that was not like other men. He was a boy in form, and an antediluvian in feature. Some thought he was a mongrel, between a Jew and an ape; some a wizard, some a kelpie, or a fairy, but most of all, that he was really and truly a Brownie. What he was I do not know, and therefore will not pretend to say; but be that as it may, in spite of locks and keys, watching and waking, the Lady of Wheelhope soon made her escape, and eloped after him. The attendants, indeed, would have made oath that she was carried away by some invisible hand, for it was impossible, they said, that she could have escaped on foot like other people; and this edition of the story took in the country; but sensible people viewed the matter in another light.

As for instance, when Wattie Blythe, the Laird's old shepherd, came in from the hill one morning, his wife Bessie thus accosted him. 'His presence be about us, Wattie Blythe! have ye heard what has happened at the ha'? Things are aye turning waur and waur there, and it looks like as if Providence had gi'en up our Laird's house to destruction. This grand estate maun now gang frae the Sprots; for it has finished them.'

'Na, na, Bessie, it isna the estate that has finished the Sprots, but the Sprots that hae finished the estate, and themsells into the boot. They hae been a wicked and degenerate race, and aye the langer the waur, till they hae reached the utmost bounds o' earthly wickedness; and it's time the deil were looking after his ain.'

'Ah, Wattie Blythe, ye never said a truer say. And that's just the very point where your story ends, and mine begins; for hasna the deil, or the fairies, or the brownies, ta'en away our Leddy bodily! and the hail country is running and riding in search o' her; and there is twenty hunder merks offered to the first that can find her, and bring her safe back. They hae ta'en her away, skin and bane, body and soul, and a', Wattie!'

'Hech-wow! but that is awesome! And where is it thought they have ta'en her to, Bessie?'

'O, they hae some guess at that frae her ain hints afore. It is thought they hae carried her after that satan of a creature, wha wrought sae muckle wae about the house. It is for him they are a' looking, for they ken weel, that where they get the tane they will get the tither.'

'Whew! is that the gate o't, Bessie? Why, then, the awfu' story is nouther mair nor less than this, that the Leddy has made a 'lopement, as they ca't, and run away after a blackguard jotteryman. Heck-wow! wae's me for human frailty! But that's just the gate! When aince the deil gets in the point o' his finger, he will soon have in his haill hand. Ay, he wants but a hair to make a tether of, ony day! I hae seen her a braw sonsy lass; but even then I feared she was devoted to destruction, for she aye mockit at religion, Bessie, and that's no a good mark of a young body. And she made a' its servants her enemies; and think you these good men's prayers were a' to blaw away i' the wind, and be nae mair regarded? Na, na, Bessie, my woman take ye this mark baithe o' our bairns and other folk's – If ever ye see a young body that disregards the Sabbath, and makes a mock at the ordinances o' religion, ye will never see that body come to muckle good. A braw hand our Leddy has made o' her gives and jeers at religion, and her mockeries o' the poor persecuted hill-folk! – sunk down by degrees into the very dregs o' sin and misery! Run away after a scullion!'

'Fy, fy, Wattie, how can ye say sae? It was weel kenn'd that she hatit him wi' a perfect and mortal hatred, and tried to make away wi' him mae ways nor ane.'

'Aha, Bessie; but nipping and scarting is Scots folk's wooing; and though it is but right that we suspend our judgments, there will naebody persuade me if she be found alang wi' the creature, but that she has run away after him in the natural way, on her twa shanks, without help either frae fairy or brownie.'

'I'll never believe sic a thing of ony woman born, let be a leddy weel up in years.'

'Od help ye, Bessie! ye dinna ken the stretch o' corrupt nature. The best o' us, when left to oursells, are nae better than strayed sheep, that will never find the way back to their ain pastures; and of a' things made o' mortal flesh, a wicked woman is the warst.'

'Alack-a-day! we got the blame o' muckle that we little deserve. But, Wattie, keep ye a geyan sharp lookout about the cleuchs and the caves o' our hope; for the Leddy kens them a' geyan weel; and gin the twenty hunder merks wad come our way, it might gang a waur gate. It wad tocher a' our bonny lasses.'

'Ay, weel I wat, Bessie, that's nae lee. And now, when ye bring me amind o't, I'm sair mista'en if I didna hear a creature up in the Brockholes this morning, skirling as if something

21

were cutting its throat. It gars a' the hairs stand on my head when I think it may hae been our Leddy, and the droich of a creature murdering her. I took it for a battle of wulcats, and wished they might pu' out ane anither's thrapples; but when I think on it again, they war unco like some o' our Leddy's unearthly screams.'

'His presence be about us, Wattie! Haste ye – pit on your bonnet – tak' your staff in your hand, and gang and see what it is.'

'Shame fa' me, if I daur gang, Bessie.'

'Hout, Wattie, trust in the Lord.'

'Aweel, sae I do. But ane's no to throw himsell ower a linn, and trust that the Lord will kep him in a blanket. And it's nae muckle safer for an auld stiff man like me to gang away out to a wild remote place, where there is ae body murdering another. What is that I hear, Bessie? Haud the lang tongue o' you, and rin to the door, and see what noise that is.'

Bessie ran to the door, but soon returned, with her mouth wide open, and her eyes set in her head.

'It is them, Wattie! it is them! His presence be about us! What will we do?'

'Them? whaten them?'

'Why, that blackguard creature, coming here, leading our Leddy by the hair o' the head, and yerking her wi' a stick. I am terrified out o' my wits. What will we do?'

'We'll *see* what they *say,*' said Wattie, manifestly in as great terror as his wife; and by a natural impulse, or as a last resource, he opened the Bible, not knowing what he did, then hurried on his spectacles; but before he got two leaves turned over, the two entered, a frightful-looking couple indeed. Merodach, with his old withered face, and ferret eyes, leading the Lady of Wheelhope by the long hair, which was mixed with grey, and whose face was all bloated with wounds and bruises, and having stripes of blood on her garments.

'How's this! – How's this, sirs?' said Wattie Blythe.

'Close that book, and I will tell you, goodman,' said Merodach.

'I can hear what you hae to say wi' the beuk open, sir,' said Wattie, turning over the leaves, pretending to look for some particular passage, but apparently not knowing what he was doing. 'It is a shamefu' business this; but some will hae to answer for't. My Leddy, I am unco grieved to see you in sic a plight. Ye hae surely been dooms sair left to yoursell.'

The Lady shook her head, uttered a feeble hollow laugh, and fixed her eyes on Merodach. But such a look! It almost frightened the simple aged couple out of their senses. It was not a look of love nor of hatred exclusively; neither was it of desire or disgust, but it was a combination of them all. It was such a look as one fiend would cast on another, in whose everlasting destruction he rejoiced. Wattie was glad to take his eyes from such countenances, and look into the Bible, that firm foundation of all his hopes and all his joy.

'I request that you will shut that book, sir,' said the horrible creature; 'or if you do not, I will shut it for you with a vengeance'; and with that he seized it, and flung it against the wall. Bessie uttered a scream, and Wattie was quite paralysed; and although he seemed disposed to run after his best friend, as he called it, the hellish looks of the Brownie interposed, and glued him to his seat.

'Hear what I have to say first,' said the creature, 'and then pore your fill on that precious book of yours. One concern at a time is enough. I came to do you a service. Here, take this cursed, wretched woman, whom you style your Lady, and deliver her up to the lawful authorities, to be restored to her husband and her place in society. She has followed one that hates her, and never said one kind word to her in his life; and though I have beat her like a dog, still she clings to me, and will not depart, so enchanted is she with the laudable purpose of cutting my throat. Tell your master and her brother, that I am not to be burdened with their maniac. I have scourged – I have spurned and kicked her, afflicting her night and day, and yet from my side she will not depart. Take her. Claim the reward in full, and your fortune is made; and so farewell!'

The creature went away, and the moment his back was turned, the Lady fell a-screaming and struggling, like one in an agony, and, in spite of all the couple's exertions, she forced herself out of their hands, and ran after the retreating Merodach. When he saw better would not be, he turned upon her, and, by one blow with his stick, struck her down; and, not content with that, continued to maltreat her in such a manner, as to all appearance would have killed twenty ordinary persons. The poor devoted dame could do nothing, but now and then utter a squeak like a half-worried cat, and writhe and grovel on the sward, till Wattie and his wife came up, and withheld her tormentor from further violence. He then bound her hands behind her back with a strong cord, and delivered her once more to the charge of the old couple, who contrived to hold her by that means, and take her home.

Wattie was ashamed to take her into the hall, but led her into one of the out-houses, whither he brought her brother to receive her. The man of the law was manifestly vexed at her reappearance, and scrupled not to testify his dissatisfaction; for when Wattie told him how the wretch had abused his sister, and that, had it not been for Bessie's interference and his own, the Lady would have been killed outright, he said, 'Why, Walter, it is a great pity that he did *not* kill her outright. What good can her life now do to her, or of what value is her life to any creature living? After one has lived to disgrace all connected with them, the sooner they are taken off the better.'

The man, however, paid old Walter down his two thousand merks, a great fortune for one like him in those days; and not to dwell longer on this unnatural story, I shall only add, very shortly, that the Lady of Wheelhope soon made her escape once more, and flew, as if drawn by an irresistible charm, to her tormentor. Her friends looked no more after her; and the last time she was seen alive, it was following the uncouth creature up the water of Daur, weary, wounded, and lame, while he was all the way beating her, as a piece of excellent amusement. A few days after that, her body was found among some wild haggs, in a place called Crook-burn, by a party of the persecuted Covenanters that were in hiding there, some of the very men whom she had exerted herself to destroy, and who had been driven, like David of old, to pray for a curse and earthly punishment upon her. They buried her like a dog at the Yetts of Keppel, and rolled three huge stones upon her grave, which are lying there to this day. When they found her corpse, it was mangled and wounded in a most shocking manner, the fiendish creature having manifestly tormented her to death. He was never more seen or heard of in this kingdom, though all that countryside was kept in terror of him for many years afterwards; and to this day, they will tell you of THE BROWNIE OF THE BLACK HAGGS, which title he seems to have acquired after his disappearance.